TO THE RESCUE

TO THE RESCUE

HOPE IRVIN MARSTON

ILLUSTRATED WITH PHOTOGRAPHS

COBBLEHILL BOOKS

DUTTON   NEW YORK

Published in the United States by Cobblehill Books, an affiliate of Dutton Children's Books, a division of Penguin Books USA Inc.
Designed by Jean Krulis
Printed in Hong Kong
First Edition   10 9 8 7 6 5 4 3 2 1

Library of Congress Cataloging-in-Publication Data
Marston, Hope Irvin.
To the rescue / Hope Irvin Marston.
p.   cm.
Includes index.
Summary: Describes how rescue workers rush to accident scenes and use special medical skills and equipment to help save the lives of badly injured people.
ISBN 0-525-65059-8
1. Rescue work—Juvenile literature. 2. Emergency medical services—Juvenile literature. [1. Rescue work. 2. Emergency medical services.] I. Title.
RA645.5.M37 1991 362.1′8—dc20 90-2575
CIP   AC

For Marcia, Shirley, and Harriet . . .
with appreciation for countless rescues
made on my behalf.

The author wishes to thank the following for their generous assistance in the preparation of this book: Rosemary LaLone, RN; Patricia Odell, secretary to the president, Medical Coaches, Incorporated; Bruce and Charmaine Wright and Rolly Churchill of Guilfoyle Ambulance Service; and Bill Lamb, Don Jennings, and Don Kane of the Black River (New York) Ambulance Squad.

Screeching brakes . . . Shattering glass . . . Crunching metal . . . Screams of pain. These are the sounds that fill the air when an accident happens.

Someone is injured every twenty seconds in the United States. This year 48,000 people will die in highway accidents. More than 11,000 will lose their lives in falls. About 6,000 will drown. There will be 5,000 deaths from fires and burns. These figures would be even higher if no one hurried to the rescue.

Policemen, firemen, and ambulances hasten to the scene when an accident occurs. They bring emergency medical personnel to aid the injured—paramedics or EMTs (Emergency Medical Technicians). Rescue workers are summoned by hospitals, public and private ambulance services, fire departments, or the police.

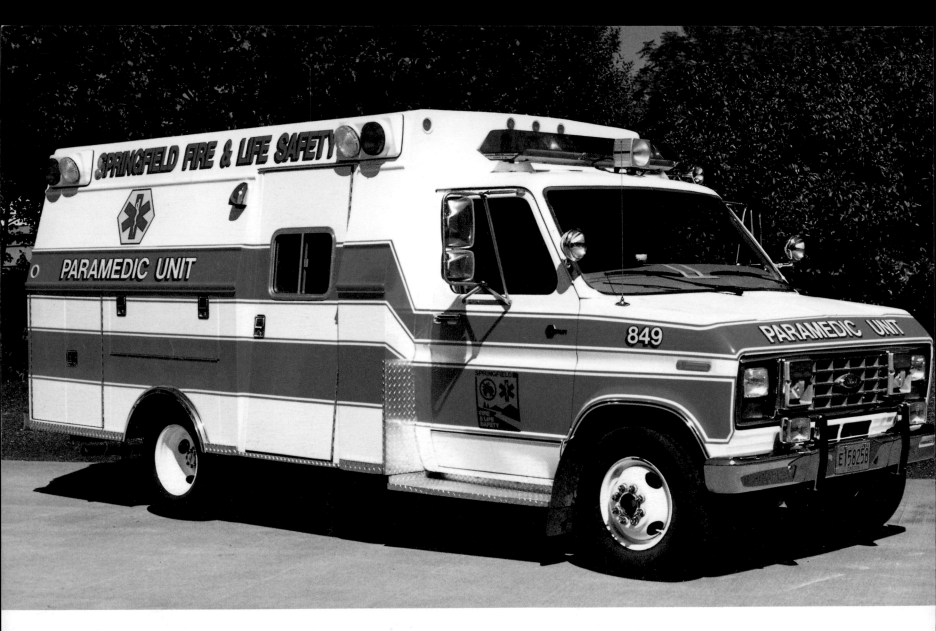

Ambulances are vehicles used to carry injured persons to a
hospital. Many ambulances are box-shaped like this one. Others
look more like a van.

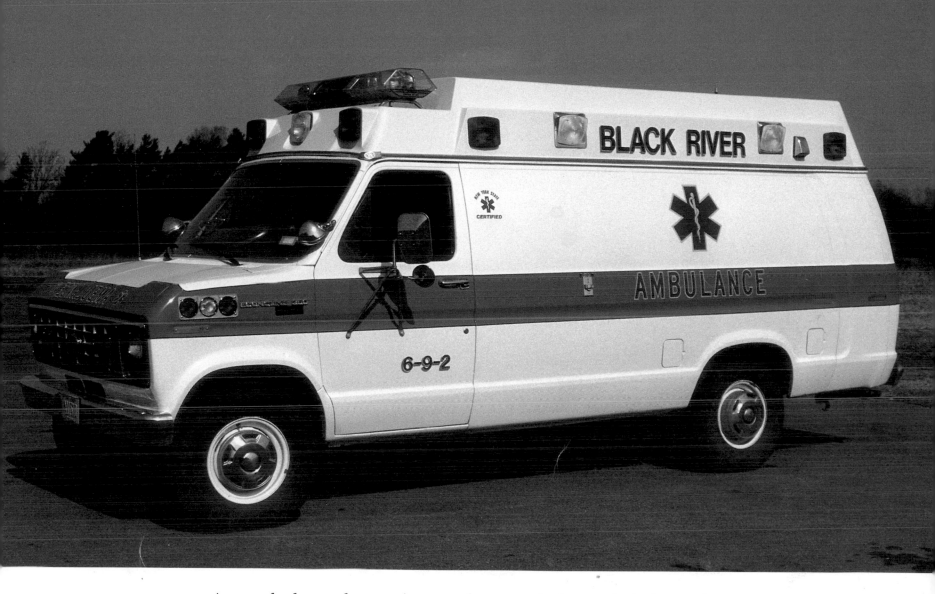

An ambulance has a siren to let people know it is hurrying to
the rescue. When other drivers hear the siren, the law says they
must pull over and stop until the ambulance passes by.

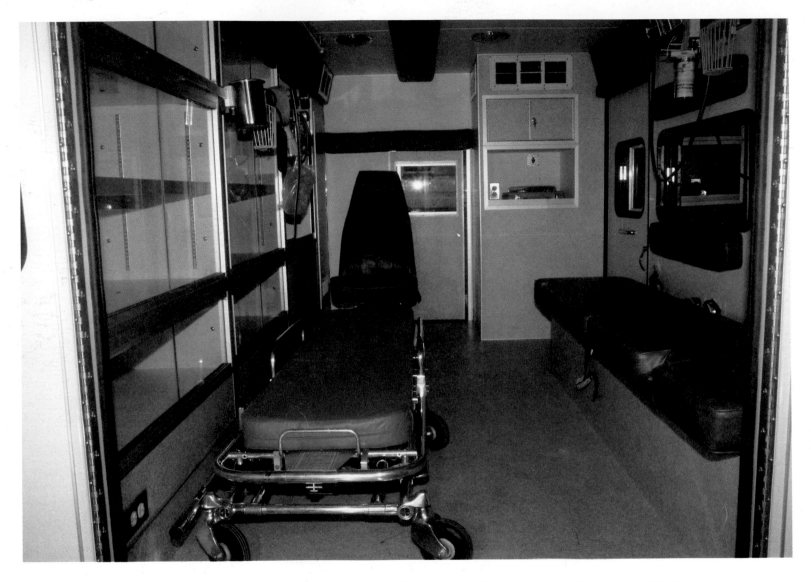

Most ambulances have a walk-through door to the cab. This allows the driver to get to the back quickly, so he can assist.

Accidents can happen anywhere at any time. Radio communication enables the rescuers to arrive promptly with the necessary equipment.

Many ambulances have words like AMBULANCE (ECNALUBMA) or RESCUE (EUCSER) spelled backwards on the front of their vehicles. That is so the word will be spelled correctly when you see it in your rearview mirror.

All rescue crews offer Basic Life Support (BLS). They are trained to stop bleeding, keep the patient breathing, and keep his heart pumping until he can be taken to the hospital.

A number of ambulances are equipped to give Advanced Life Support (ALS). Highly trained paramedics treat the seriously injured patient on the spot because he or she might die before they can get the victim to the hospital. They provide the kind of care one would receive in an emergency room. They give IVs, if needed. IV means "intravenous." A needle is inserted in a vein to supply liquid food to the patient. Only ALS personnel may give injections or drugs.

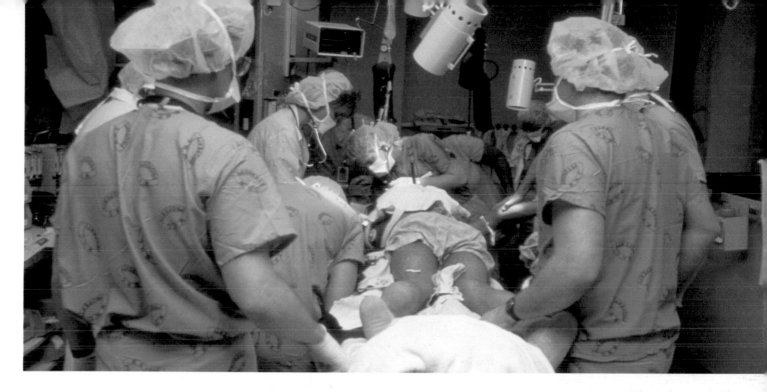

To save lives, it is important that seriously injured patients be treated during the "golden hour." That is the first hour following their accident. Whether an accident victim recovers or dies is often due to the speed and skill with which he is treated.

"Trauma" means any injury. But severe trauma can produce shock, a condition that occurs if there is not enough blood flowing through the body. A great loss of blood pressure and a slowing down of breathing and heartbeat are signs of shock. To reverse shock, the patient must be rushed to a hospital, or a trauma center, where a skilled staff can treat him during his "golden hour."

Equipment for Basic Life Support includes anti-shock trousers. The trousers force the blood from the lower half of the body to the upper half where the vital organs, like the heart, are located.

Sometimes accident victims are trapped in their cars. A hydraulic spreader . . .

. . . or cutter may be needed to free them.

People are sometimes trapped under heavy objects like over-turned tractors, trailers, or railroad cars. They can be rescued by lifting the heavy object with bags filled with compressed air. Empty air bags need little clearance when placed under an object. They can be stacked on top of one another to lift many tons. One kind is this MatJack.

All rescue vehicles carry different kinds of splints to protect arms, legs, or entire bodies. A full-body splint can serve as a stretcher to carry the patient to the ambulance.

Patients are moved on stretchers to prevent further injury. This one, called a Sked, is a three-by-eight-foot sheet of plastic that wraps around the patient.

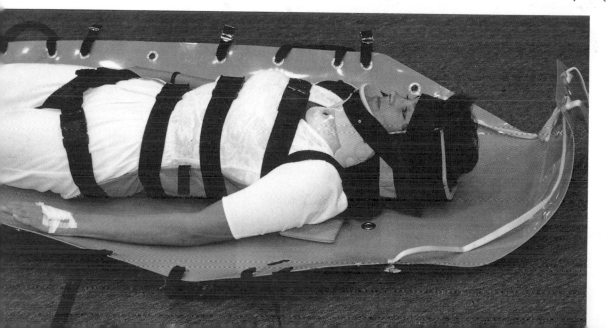

17

A Sked allows the patient to be carried safely through narrow spaces like a mine shaft . . .

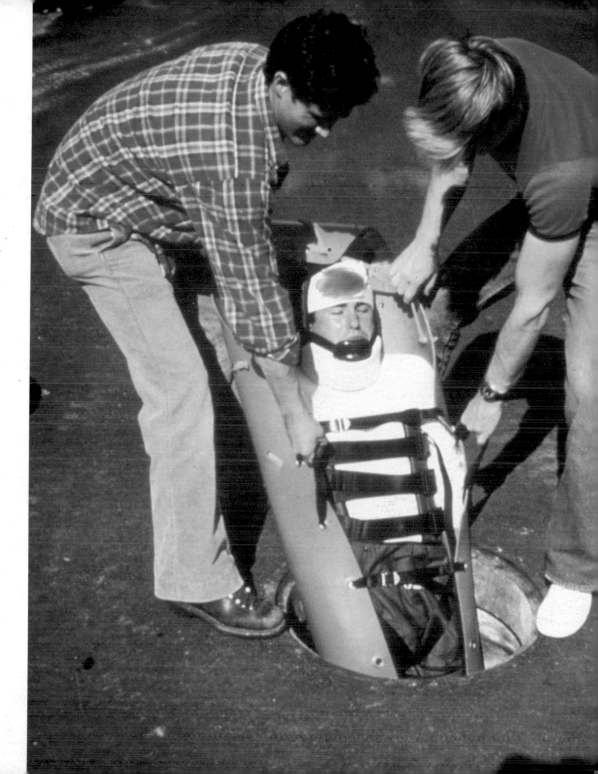

. . . or a manhole.

In areas where accidents are likely to happen in the water, the police department or the fire department may have a trained Dive Rescue team. These teams are dispatched by the police or firemen who assist the rescue operations on land.

An inflatable boat makes a dandy ambulance.

Search and Rescue (SAR) is carried out by the military, the state police, the National Park Service, or voluntary organizations. The purpose is to find lost people or clues to their whereabouts. Search and Rescue workers look for children who have wandered away from a campsite, lost hunters, downed airplanes, missing ships.

Helicopters with special equipment are often used in these searches. This equipment might include a public-address and siren system or searchlights for surveying areas. There are litters, sand filters, or an electric hoist for use in places where the helicopter can't land.

Search and Rescue teams spend many hours practicing their maneuvers.

Large airports use a special kind of fire truck called a Crash Fire Rescue vehicle (CFR). The CFR carries foam and chemicals to put out airplane fires. A CFR truck has a roof-mounted turret gun. As the truck approaches the fire, the turret gun shoots out chemicals. The fire must be put out before anyone can approach to rescue the injured.

Firemen often endanger themselves to save others. At least 100,000 firemen will be injured this year in the line of duty and more than 100 will die "with their boots on." Ambulances are sent to the rescue at fires to help the fire fighters as well as the fire victims.

Animals have accidents, too. It's less frightening to them when they can be treated at home. But if they need difficult surgery or long-term treatment, they have to be taken to an animal hospital or clinic. Some organizations have animal ambulances for this purpose. Senior citizens, handicapped folk, and those without cars may need an ambulance for a sick pet.

Equine ambulances for injured horses are used at race tracks in some states. These ambulances are well padded, so that the horses will not suffer more injury on the way to the animal hospital.

When speed is important because of the kind of injury, the nature of the illness, or the distance to the hospital, patients are carried by air. Helicopters, turboprops, or jet planes are used. These air ambulances are dispatched by hospitals, the state police, county sheriffs, or MAST (a helicopter service for military personnel and civilians living near an army installation).

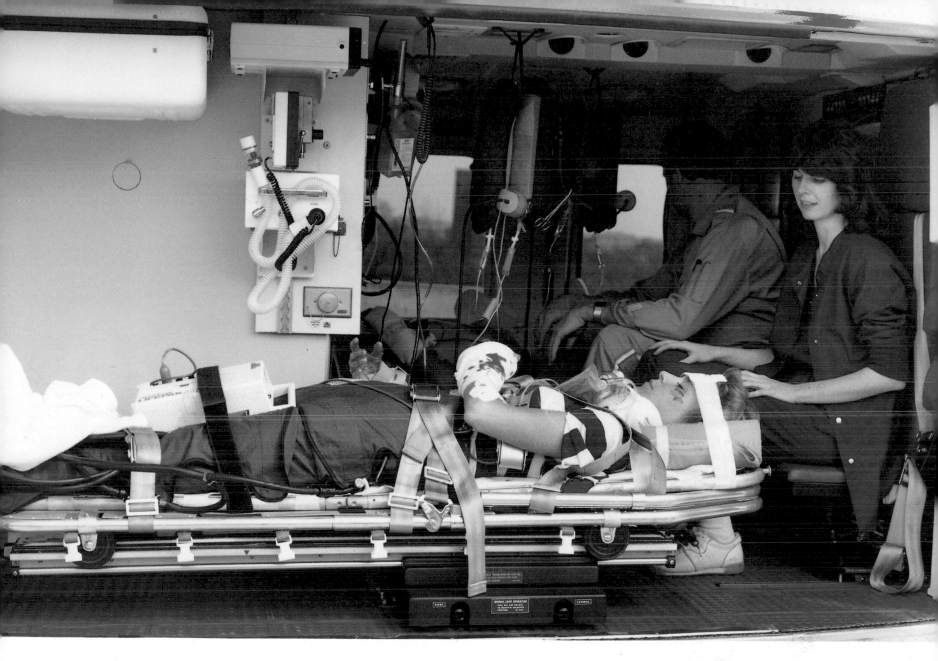

Medical helicopters have wide doors to make loading easier.

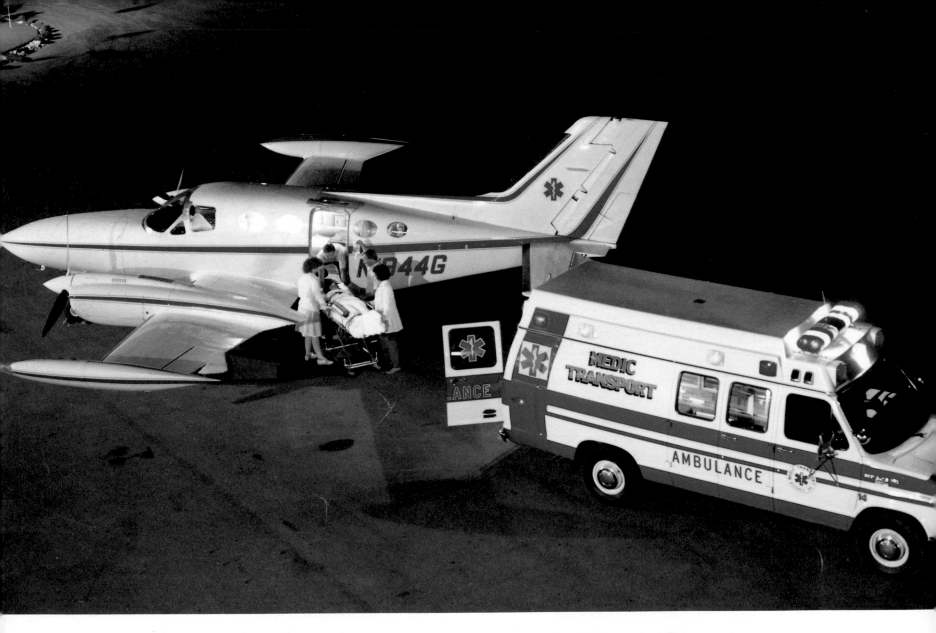

Trained medical personnel make gentle, but speedy, transfers
from ground ambulances to air ambulances.

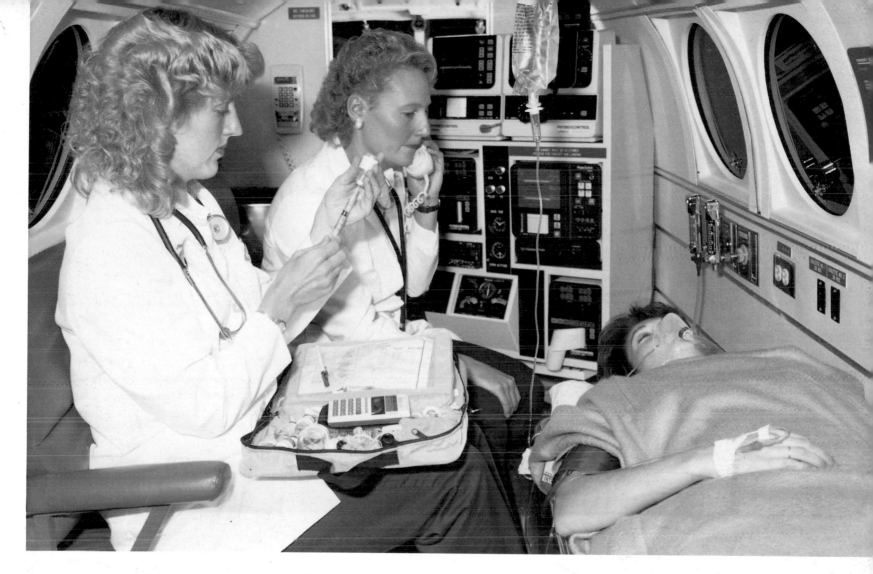

Airplanes equipped to provide Advanced Life Support are found at major medical centers around the world. They are staffed by skilled medical workers, who play an important part in saving lives.

In the United States each year more people die from drowning than in fires. Some localities near waterways provide Harbor Patrols to assist when there are water accidents.

This Yankee Airboat was designed to carry out rescue operations on the rivers, lakes, and marshlands of the Northeast.

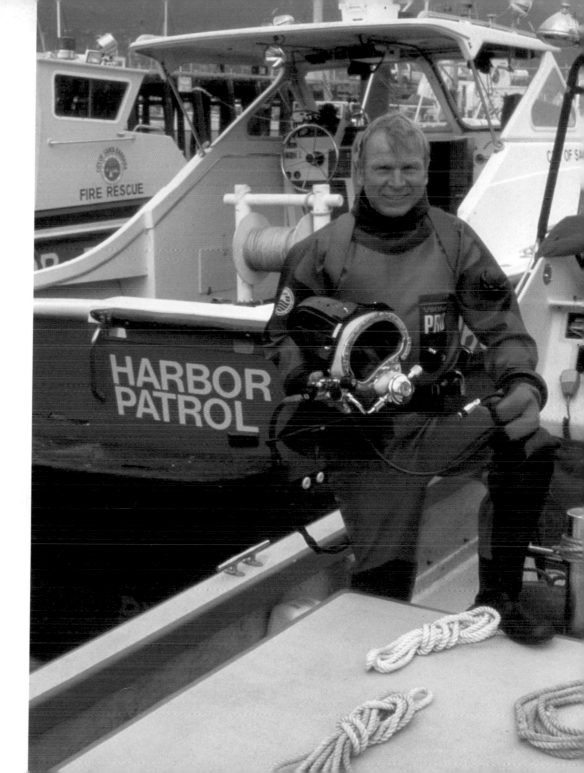

The Harbor Patrol helps victims of swimming or boating accidents. In deep water the services of a diver may be needed.

The U.S. Coast Guard spends about one-fourth of its time carrying out Search and Rescue operations. It uses short-range helicopters, as well as patrol boats. Most of the distress calls it receives come from recreational boaters.

Deep-sea rescue depends on boats and helicopters strong enough to survive terrible storms and dangerous currents. It also depends on brave men. When the Coast Guard receives a distress call, it must decide which service to use.

If speed is important, a helicopter will be sent. On the other hand, a motor lifeboat can stay out longer without refueling. It can take people off ships which a helicopter could not get near because of masts, rigging, fire, or wind. It is better-equipped to carry out night searches than a helicopter. But a long search for a missing ship can best be carried out by an airplane.

The Deep Submergence Rescue Vehicle (DSRV) is a cigar-shaped submersible built to rescue nuclear submarines. It "mates" with the submarine to let the crew transfer to the DSRV.

Farming is the most dangerous occupation in America in terms of accidental injuries and deaths. In at least three states, there are programs to train Emergency Medical Service (EMS) workers in how to handle farm accidents.

In New York State, FARMEDIC trains farmers, their wives and children, and EMS personnel. Iowa and North Dakota also have EMS farm safety programs.

Each year about 300 children in America die from accidents on farms. Injuries occur when an arm or leg or sleeve gets caught in a piece of machinery. Lots of accidents happen when children fall off tractors or the tractors overturn.

Many children have accidents. If you have one, you may be whisked into an ambulance by uniformed strangers. The wailing siren may terrify you. You won't be so frightened if you know what to expect. The ambulance attendants will calm your fears.

Some fire departments have programs to teach children about ambulances and rescue operations. In Frederick, Maryland, the Junior Fire Company No. 2, gives an ambulance tour to kids. The ambulance is driven to the mall. Then children are invited to come in and look around.

When you step inside, a friendly paramedic answers your questions. He lets you handle some of the equipment. He tells you how it helps you if you are in an accident.

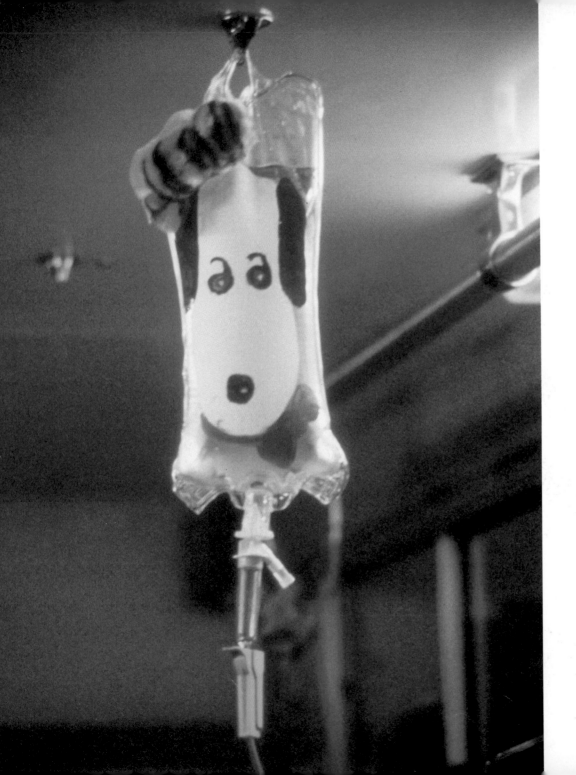

Inside the ambulance
you will see some old
friends. Snoopy and Gar-
field hang from an IV bag,
which is used to feed people intravenously.

Mickey Mouse is there wearing a leg splint.

Robots can teach you about accidents, too. Police and firemen throughout the United States take talking "officers" like these to schools. The robots teach boys and girls what to do in case of an accident. They also talk about seat belts and bicycle safety.

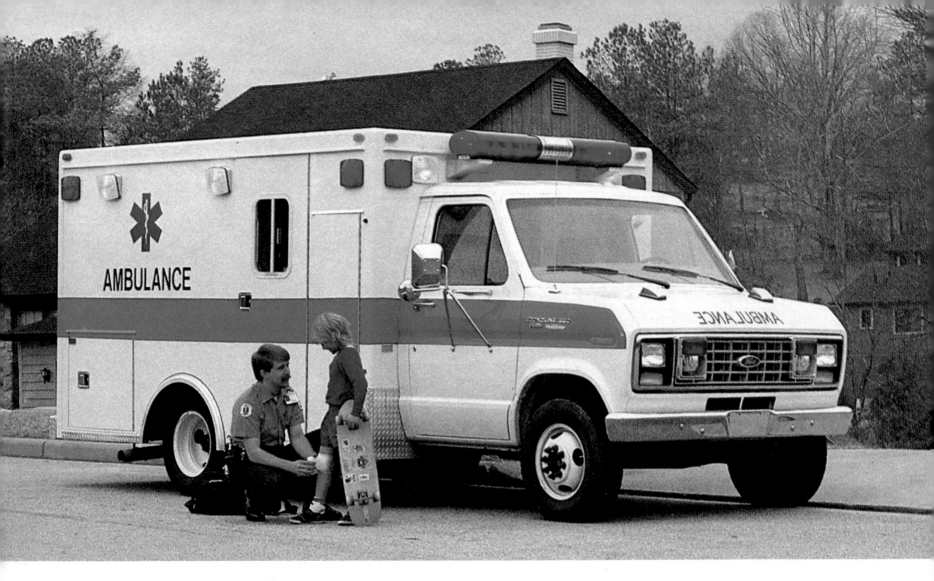

Here's hoping you do not have an accident. If you do, don't be frightened. There are lots of trained people who will come to your rescue. The policemen, firemen, and ambulance crews are your friends.

INDEX